Real Sisters Pretend

Author's Note

One day I overheard two of my daughters at play, and while they pretended to hike up a mountain with their stuffed animals, they revisited a question a stranger had asked them: "Are you *real* sisters?" They were baffled. They understood "real" as the opposite of "pretend," and they knew they never had to pretend to be sisters. As they climbed pretend mountains that day, they talked about how adoption made them "real sisters" even though they have different birthparents and even though they don't look alike, and I was proud of the ways they took care of one another in their play and in their conversation.

As Tayja says in the story, sometimes people don't "understand about adoption" and might wrongly think that "real sisters" must have the same birthparents. In our family, we understand that being biologically related is not the only way to be a "real" family. We understand that adoption is another way adults become parents and children become daughters and sons, and, maybe, sisters and brothers. And we understand that the often complex circumstances behind the need for adoption require respect for birth families and include diverse stories of love, loss, choice, and hardship—stories belonging first and foremost to adopted children themselves.

Sometimes there are many people in a family, sometimes just a few. A child might have only sisters, or only brothers, or stepsiblings, or no siblings at all. Kids might have one mom and one dad, or stepparents, or two moms, or two dads, or just one parent. Some kids have caregivers who aren't their parents. Some adopted children have relationships with their birth families, while others do not. Some children live with foster families who care for them until they can safely go home to biological family members or until an adoption plan or another plan is in place for them. And there are also the many possibilities for aunties and uncles, grandparents and cousins, and all the other people who can be in families.

No matter how a family comes to be or who is or isn't in it, the most important thing is for everyone to feel loved, safe, and cared for. Every child needs and deserves a forever family, and there are thousands of children in the United States alone who are waiting to be adopted. I feel so lucky to be a mom to six amazing children. One of the most wonderful parts about raising my family has been seeing the great love that my sons and daughters share as siblings. Some of them are biologically related to one another and some are not, but because of adoption they are all real sisters and brothers, and they always will be.

—Megan Dowd Lambert

Real Sisters Pretend

Megan Dowd Lambert

Illustrated by Nicole Tadgell

TILBURY HOUSE
PUBLISHERS

Tilbury House Publishers
12 Starr Street
Thomaston, Maine 04861
www.tilburyhouse.com

Hardcover ISBN 978-0-88448-441-7
eBook ISBN 978-0-88448-497-4
Paperback ISBN 978-0-88448-784-5

Cloth: 15 16 17 18 19 20 XXX 10 9 8 7 6 5 4 3
Paper: 15 16 17 18 19 20 XXX 10 9 8 7 6 5 4 3 2 1

Library of Congress Cataloging-in-Publication Data

Names: Lambert, Megan Dowd, author. | Tadgell, Nicole, 1969- illustrator.
Title: Real sisters pretend / Megan Dowd Lambert ; illustrated by Nicole
    Tadgell.
Description: Thomaston, Maine : Tilbury House Publishers, [2016] | Summary:
    Safe in the knowledge that adoption has made them "forever family,"
    stepsisters Mia and Tayja improvise an imaginary adventure with a joyful
    homecoming to a real home with their two moms.
Identifiers: LCCN 2016000040 (print) | LCCN 2016002925 (ebook) | ISBN
    9780884484417 (hardcover) | ISBN 9780884484974 (ebook)
Subjects: | CYAC: Stepsisters--Fiction. | Adoption--Fiction. |
    Imagination—Fiction.
Classification: LCC PZ7.1.L26 Re 2016 (print) | LCC PZ7.1.L26 (ebook) | DDC
    [Fic]—dc23
LC record available at http://lccn.loc.gov/2016000040

Designed by Nicole Tadgell and Frame25 Productions

Printed in China

Dedications

For Natayja and Emilia, real sisters to each other
and to Rory, Stevie, Caroline, and Jesse too.
—M.D.L.

For Maggie.
—N.T.

And then when we went to the courthouse for your adoption day, the judge said I could make Lion bang the gavel.

But you just tried to chew it.

Like a carrot stick. And then we were *real* sisters. Even if some people don't know that.

And Momma said, "Of course they are."

And then she said that lady didn't understand about adoption.

Megan Dowd Lambert teaches in the graduate programs in Children's Literature at Simmons College. At the Eric Carle Museum of Picture Book Art she developed two original storytime models, the Whole Book Approach and A Book in Hand, which are aimed at engaging readers with the picture book as a visual art form. A frequent speaker at professional conferences, schools, libraries, and museums, she reviews children's books for *Kirkus Reviews* and the *Horn Book* and contributes to *Horn Book Magazine*'s "Books in the Home" column. A mother of six children ranging from infancy to college-aged, Megan lives with her family in Massachusetts. Her books include *A Crow of His Own* and *Reading Picture Books with Children: How to Shake Up Storytime and Get Kids Talking about What They See*. Readers can find Megan online at *http://megandowdlambert.com* or @MDowdLambert.

Nicole Tadgell's illustrations have been featured in *The Encyclopedia of Writing and Illustrating Children's Books* and in numerous exhibitions. She has taught workshops and classes at the Worcester Art Museum, the Eric Carle Museum of Picture Book Art, and at Society of Children's Book Writers and Illustrators (SCBWI) conferences. Nicole also lectures at New England schools and colleges and demonstrates the picture book process in classrooms, libraries, and bookstores. Her award-winning children's books include *First Peas to the Table*, *In the Garden with Dr. Carver*, *Lucky Beans*, and *Fatuma's New Cloth*.